He Is Risen!

Published by Concordia Publishing House
3558 S. Jefferson Avenue
St. Louis, MO 63118-3968
1-800-325-3040 • www.cph.org

Manufactured in China

1 2 3 4 5 6 7 8 9 10   16 15 14 13 12 11 10 09 08 07

Easter Is for Me!

By Dandi Daley Mackall – Illustrated by Anton Petrov

CONCORDIA PUBLISHING HOUSE • SAINT LOUIS

When Easter comes, the church bells ring.
We color eggs and dress for spring.
But listen, and I think you'll see
Why Easter is for me.

When Jesus came to live on earth
And chose a stable for His birth,
From long ago, eternity,
I think He was thinking of me.

He grew up wise and good and strong,
Obeyed His parents, did no wrong.
And while He played in Galilee,
I think He was thinking of me.

When Jesus taught and spoke God's Word,
The people heard and understood.
He told them He would set them free.
I think He was speaking to me.

He chose twelve friends and taught them well
With stories only He could tell.
Yet when they fished beside the sea,
I think He was fishing for me.

The sick were cured. The lame could run!
He loved and cared for everyone.
And when He made the blind to see,
He knew He would need to heal me.

He rode a donkey into town,
As people laid their branches down
To shouts of praise and victory.
But still, He was thinking of me.

He poured the wine and broke the bread.
"Remember Me," the Savior said.
He promised life eternally.
I know He was promising me.

Then later, Jesus knelt and prayed.
The others slept, but Jesus stayed.
And in that garden, quietly,
I know He was praying for me.

They beat Him up and knocked Him down
And mocked Him with a thorny crown.
He could have fought. He let it be.
I know He was suffering for me.

They crucified the Son of Man.
His death was part of Jesus' plan.
I can't explain the mystery.
He did what He did for me.

Christ rose again on Easter Day!
He lives to show us Jesus' way.
And so it's plain as it can be
Why Easter is for me!

Alleluia